5.6

First omnibus edition, April 2011

The Red Tree
Copyright © 2001 by Shaun Tan

The Lost Thing
Copyright © 2000 by Shaun Tan

The Rabbits
Text copyright © 1998 by Jomden Pty Ltd
Illustrations copyright © 1998 by Shaun Tan

Additional artwork copyright © 2011 by Shaun Tan
Additional text copyright © 2011 by Shaun Tan and Jomden Pty Ltd

Library of Congress Cataloging-in-Publication Data is available.
LOC number 2010030936

ISBN 978-0-545-22924-1

10 9 8 7 6 5 4 3 2 1   11 12 13 14 15

Printed in Singapore   46

The Red Tree, The Lost Thing, and The Rabbits were first published in Australia
by Lothian Books, an imprint of Hachette Australia Pty Ltd.

sometimes the day begins
with nothing to look forward to

and things go from bad to worse

darkness
overcomes you

nobody understands

the world is a

deaf machine

sometimes you wait

and wait

and wait

and wait

and wait

and wait

and wait

but nothing ever happens

wonderful things
are
passing
you
by

terrible fates are

inevitable

sometimes
you just don't know
what you are
supposed
to
do

or

who

you   meant
            are

                         to

                    be

or

where
you are

and the day seems to end
the way it began

but suddenly there it is
right in front of you

bright and vivid

quietly waiting

just as you imagined it would be

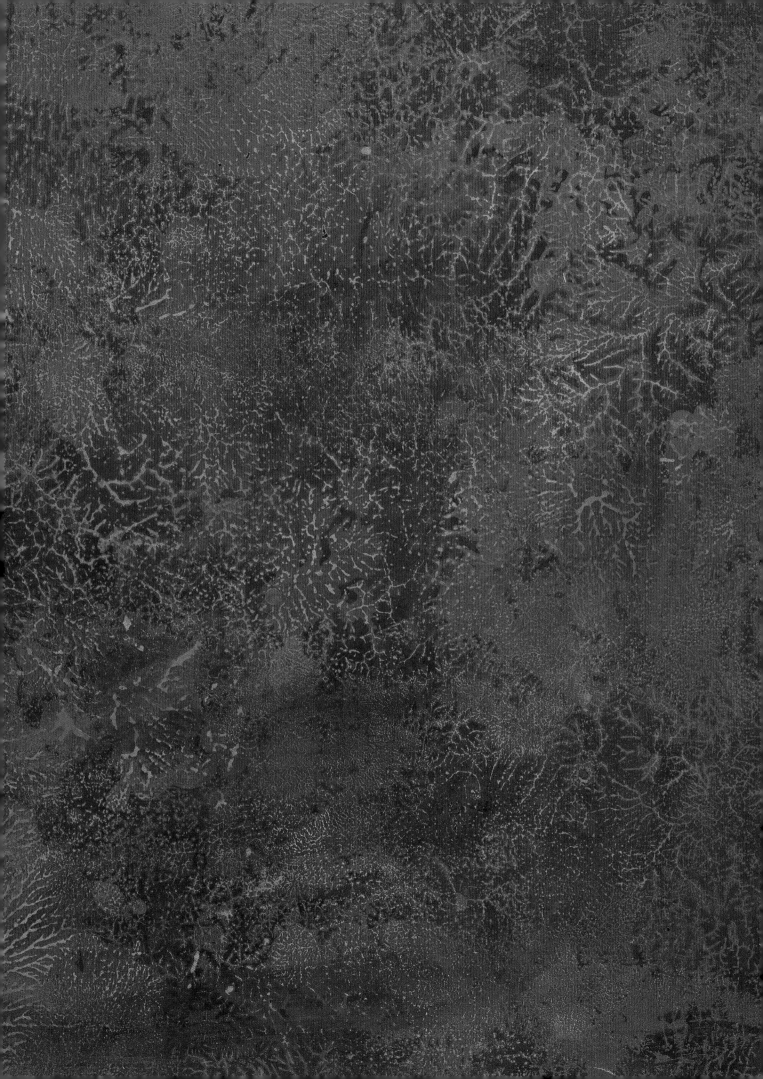

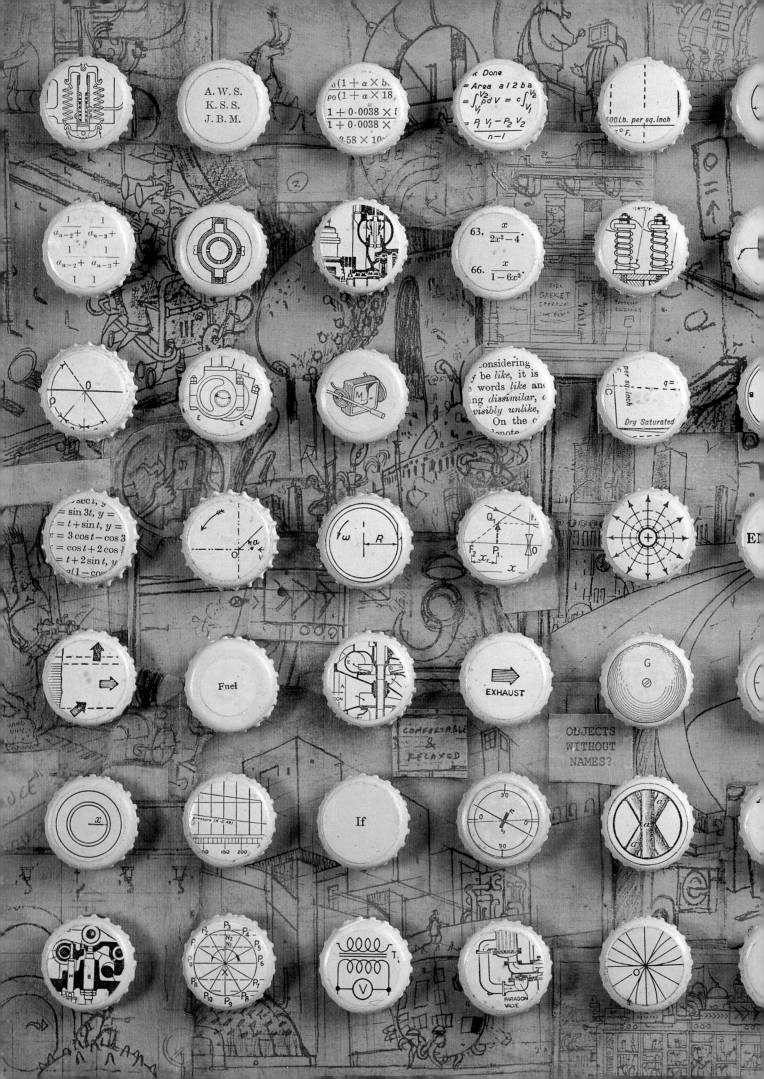

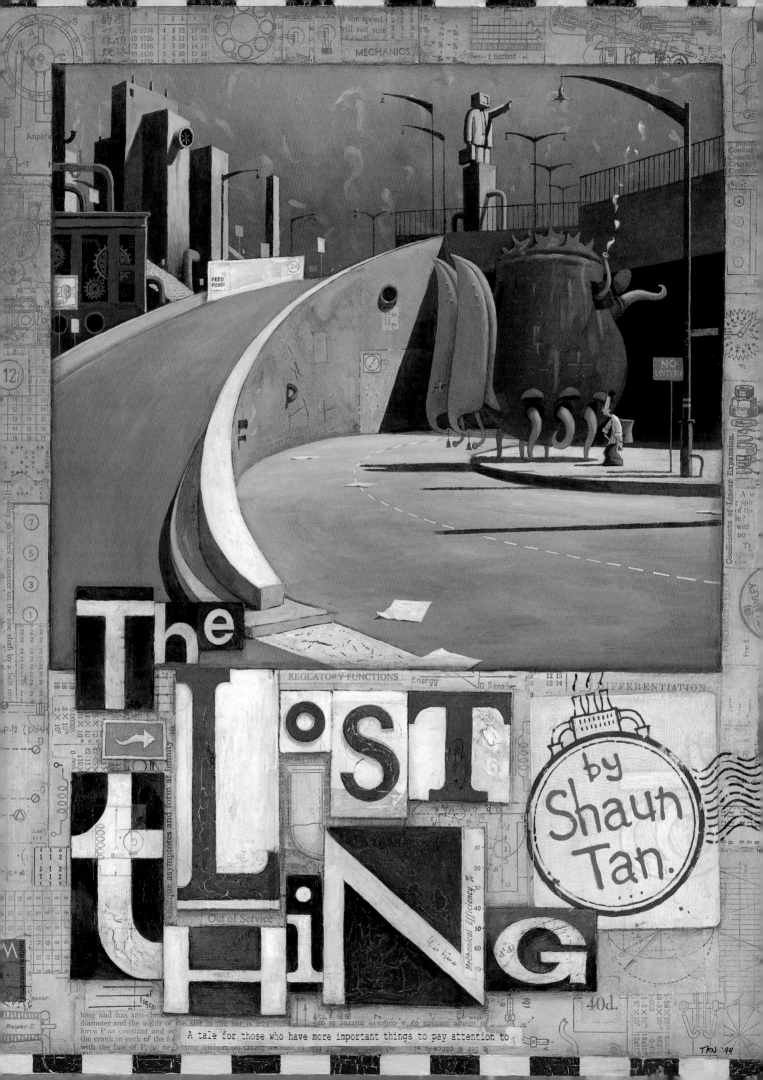

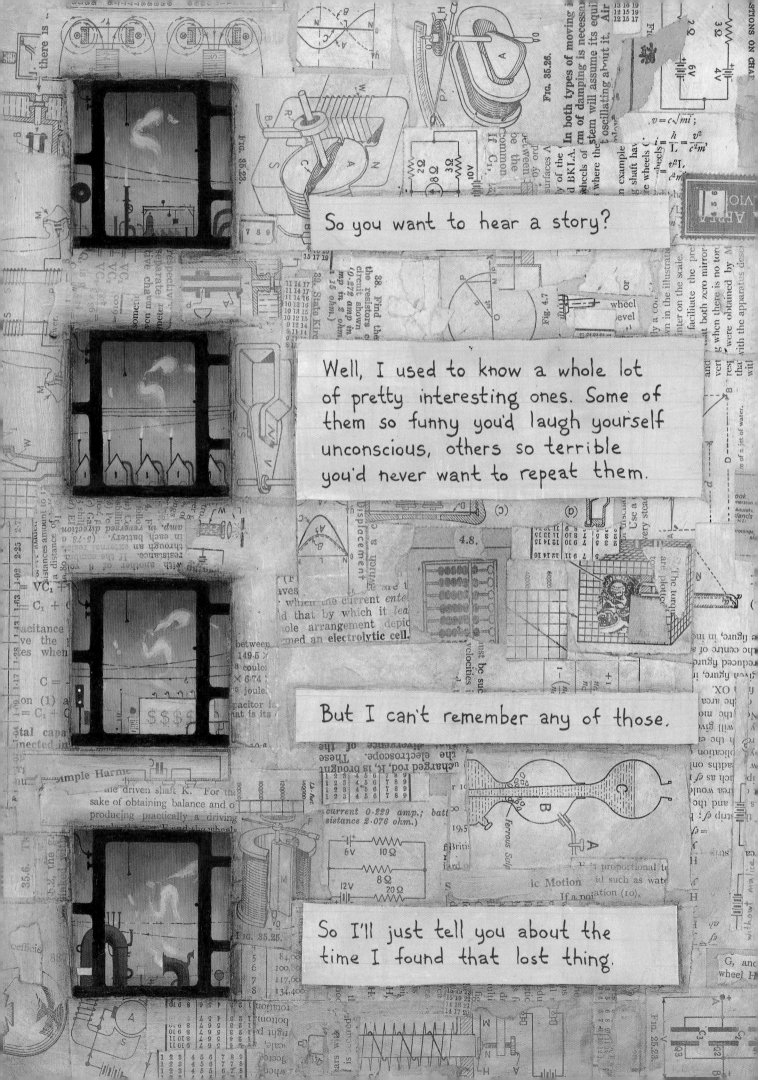

So you want to hear a story?

Well, I used to know a whole lot of pretty interesting ones. Some of them so funny you'd laugh yourself unconscious, others so terrible you'd never want to repeat them.

But I can't remember any of those.

So I'll just tell you about the time I found that lost thing.

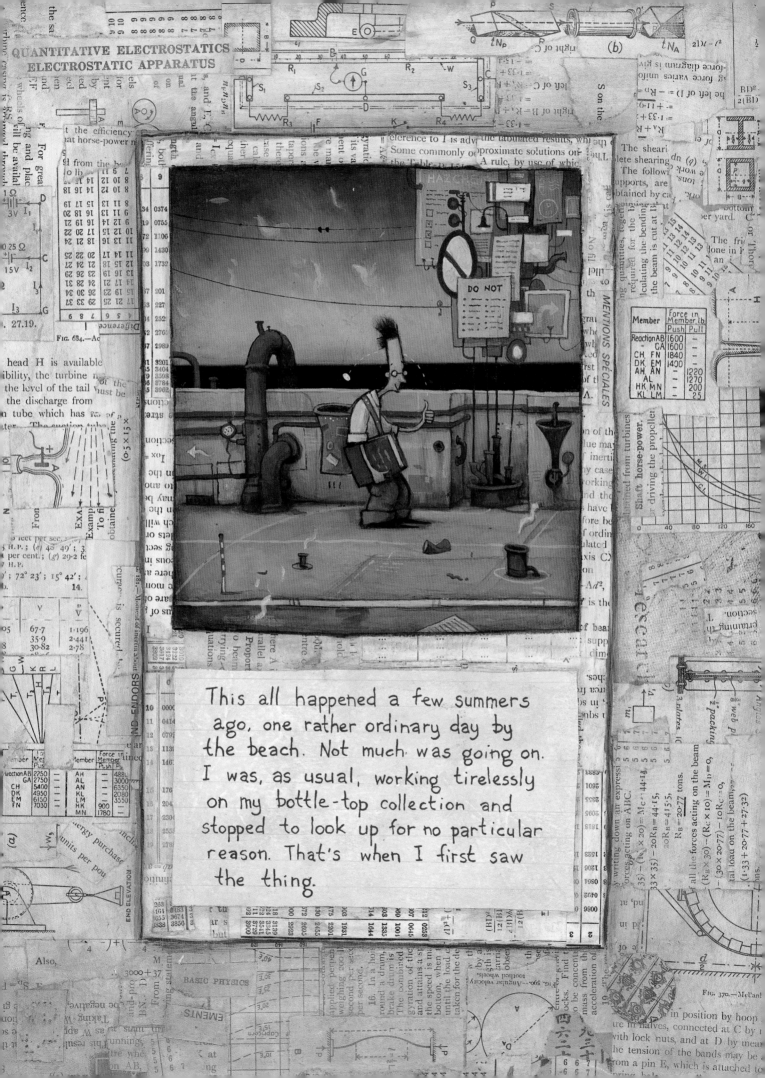

This all happened a few summers ago, one rather ordinary day by the beach. Not much was going on. I was, as usual, working tirelessly on my bottle-top collection and stopped to look up for no particular reason. That's when I first saw the thing.

I must have stared at it for a while. I mean, it had a really weird look about it — a sad, lost sort of look. Nobody else seemed to notice it was there. Too busy doing beach stuff, I guess.

It was quite friendly though, once I started talking to it.

I asked a few people if they knew anything about it, but nobody was very helpful.

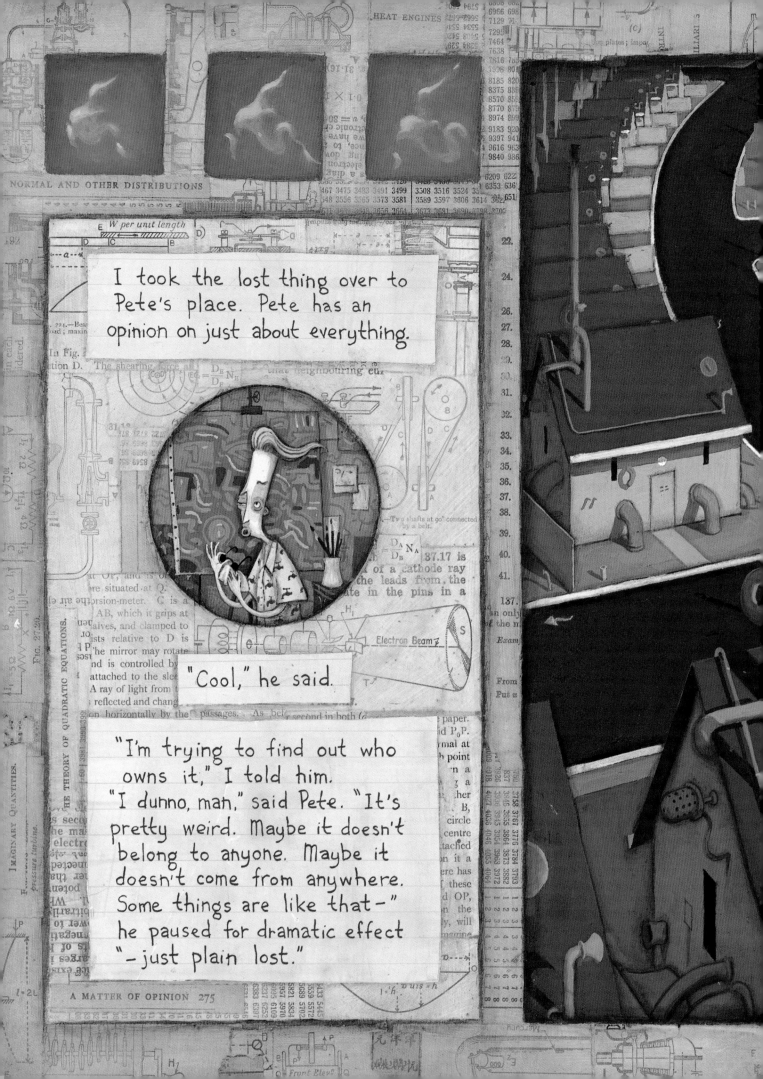

I took the lost thing over to Pete's place. Pete has an opinion on just about everything.

"Cool," he said.

"I'm trying to find out who owns it," I told him.
"I dunno, man," said Pete. "It's pretty weird. Maybe it doesn't belong to anyone. Maybe it doesn't come from anywhere. Some things are like that—" he paused for dramatic effect "—just plain lost."

There was nothing left to do but take the thing home with me. I mean, I couldn't just leave it wandering the streets. Plus I felt kind of sorry for it.

My parents didn't really notice it at first.
Too busy discussing current events, I guess.

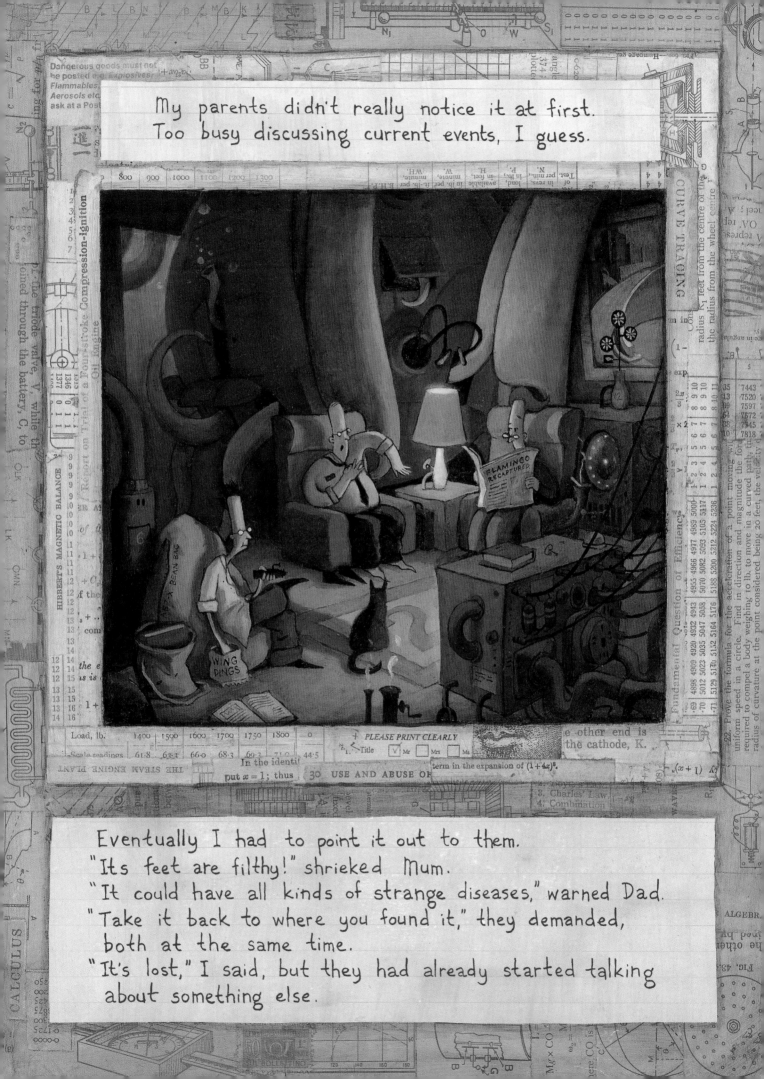

Eventually I had to point it out to them.
"It's feet are filthy!" shrieked Mum.
"It could have all kinds of strange diseases," warned Dad.
"Take it back to where you found it," they demanded,
both at the same time.
"It's lost," I said, but they had already started talking
about something else.

I hid the thing in our back shed and gave it something to eat, once I found out what it liked. It seemed a bit happier then, even though it was still lost.

I checked the local paper for any lost pet notices, but only found a lot of good deals on refrigerator repairs. I remember thinking then that Pete was probably right, that some things were just plain lost. In any case, I sure couldn't keep the thing in the shed forever. Mum or Dad would eventually notice it when they came out looking for a hammer or something.

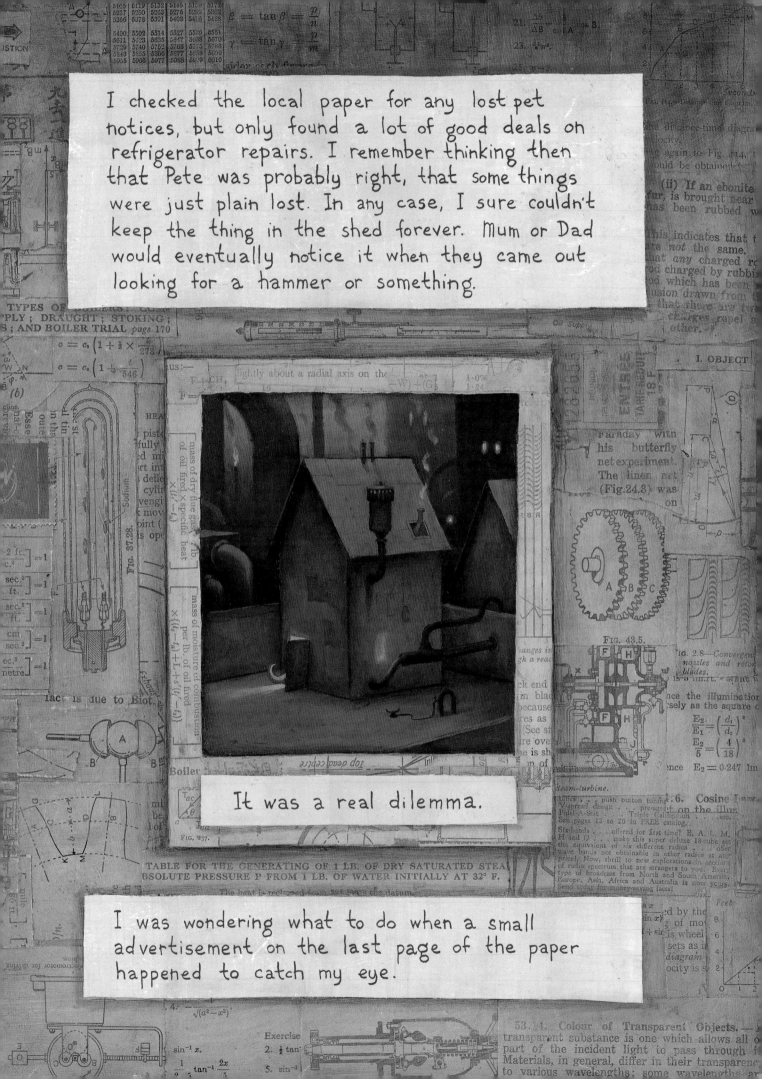

It was a real dilemma.

I was wondering what to do when a small advertisement on the last page of the paper happened to catch my eye.

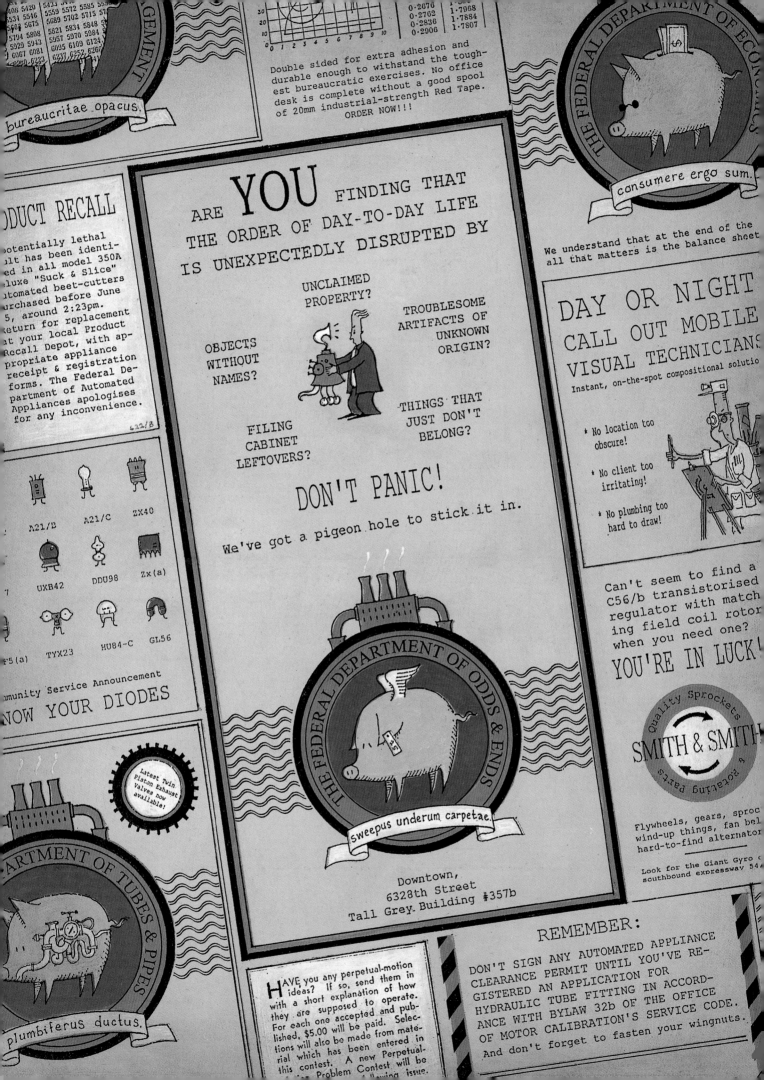

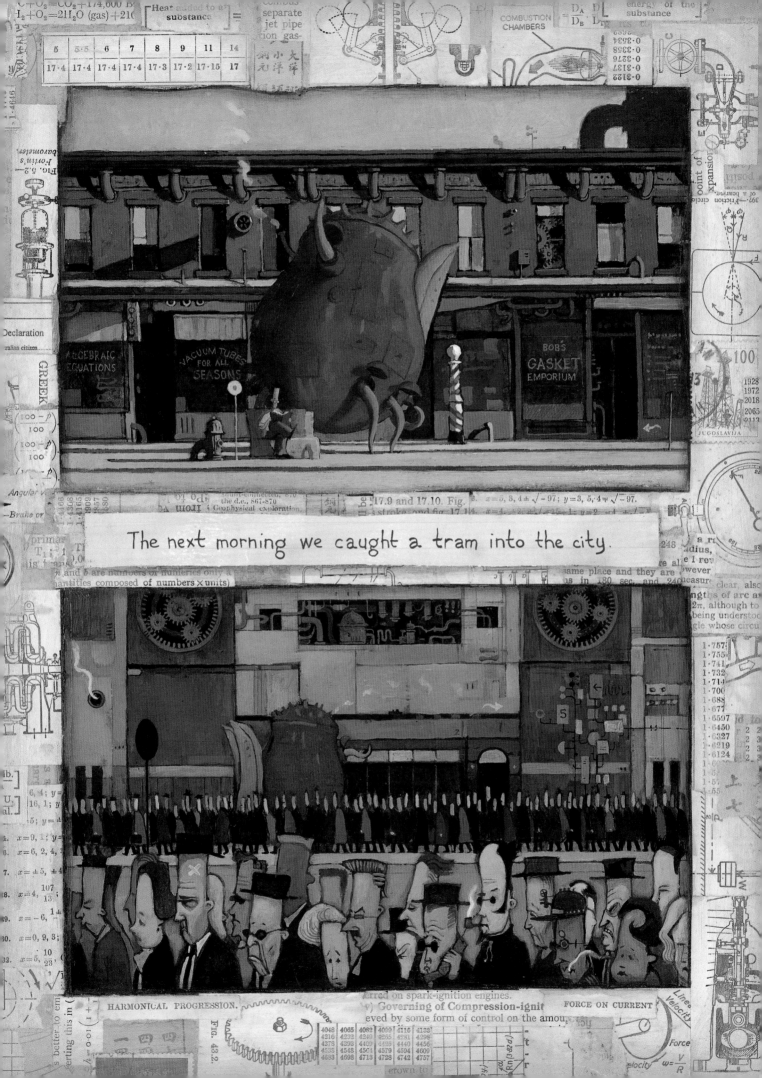

The next morning we caught a tram into the city.

We arrived at a tall grey building with no windows. It was pretty dark in there, and it smelt like disinfectant.
"I have a lost thing," I called to the receptionist at the front desk.
"Fill in these forms," she said.

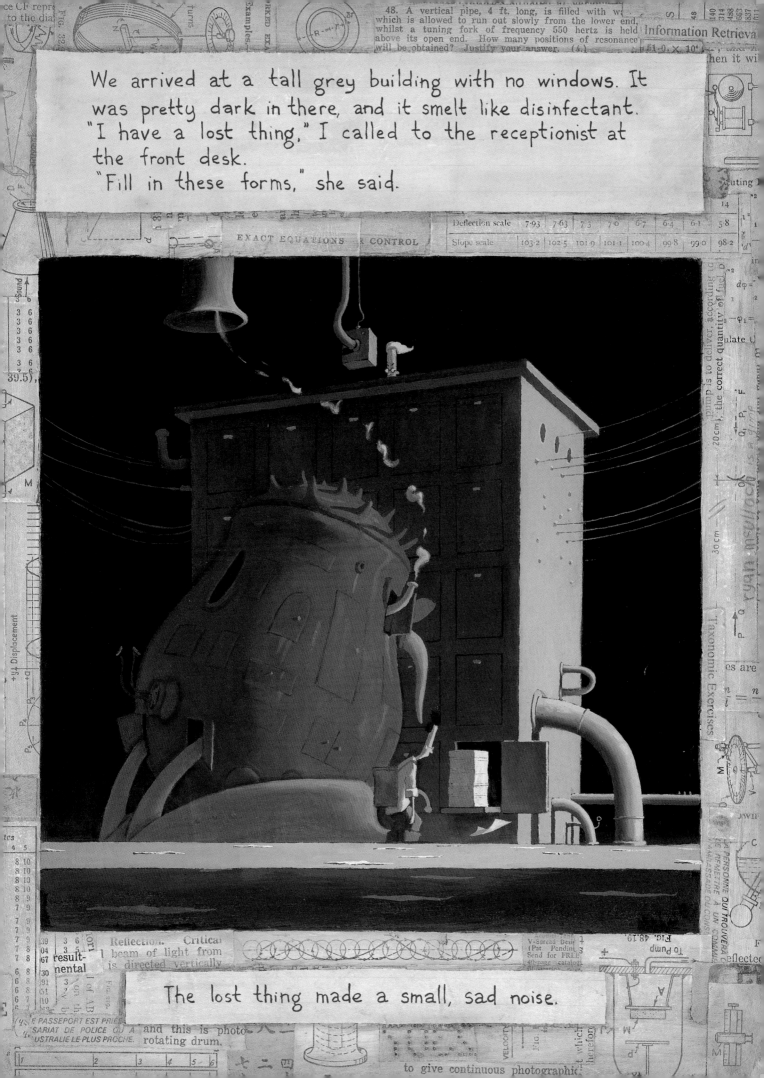

The lost thing made a small, sad noise.

I was looking around for a pen
when I felt something tug the
back of my shirt.
"If you really care about that
thing, you shouldn't leave it
here," said a tiny voice. "This
is a place for forgetting,
leaving behind, smoothing over.
Here, take this."

It was a business card with
a kind of sign on it. It wasn't
very important looking, but it
did seem to point somewhere.
"Cheers," I said.

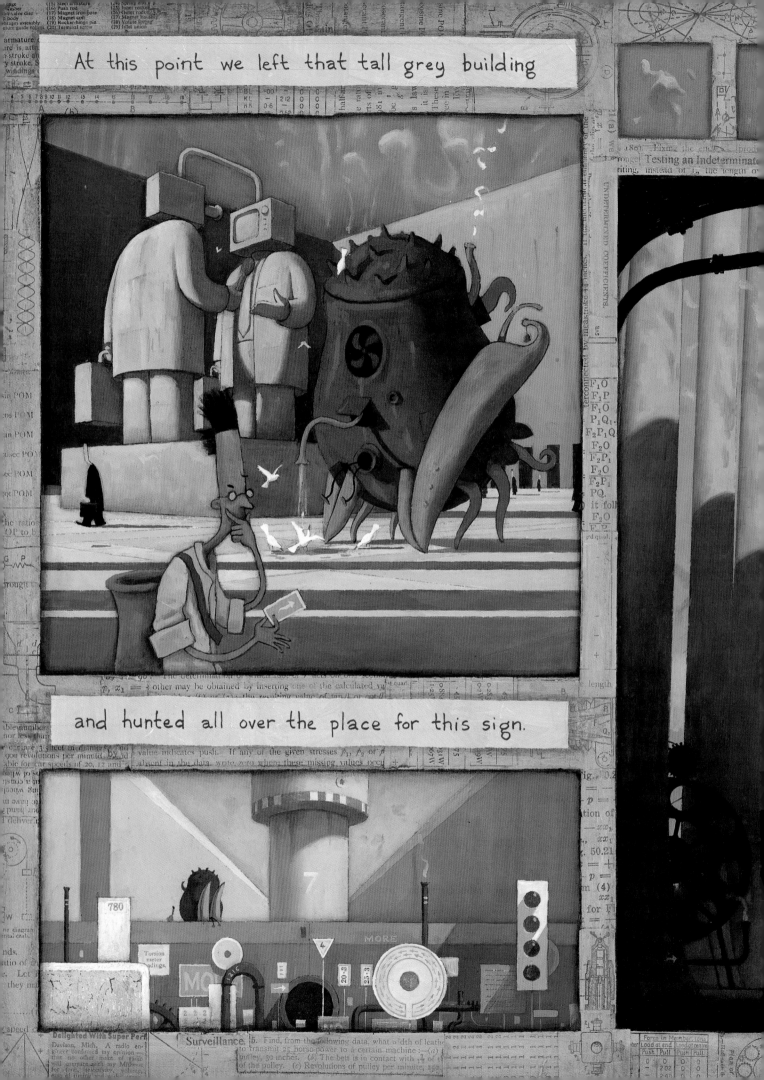

At this point we left that tall grey building

and hunted all over the place for this sign.

It wasn't an easy job,

and I can't say I knew what it all meant.

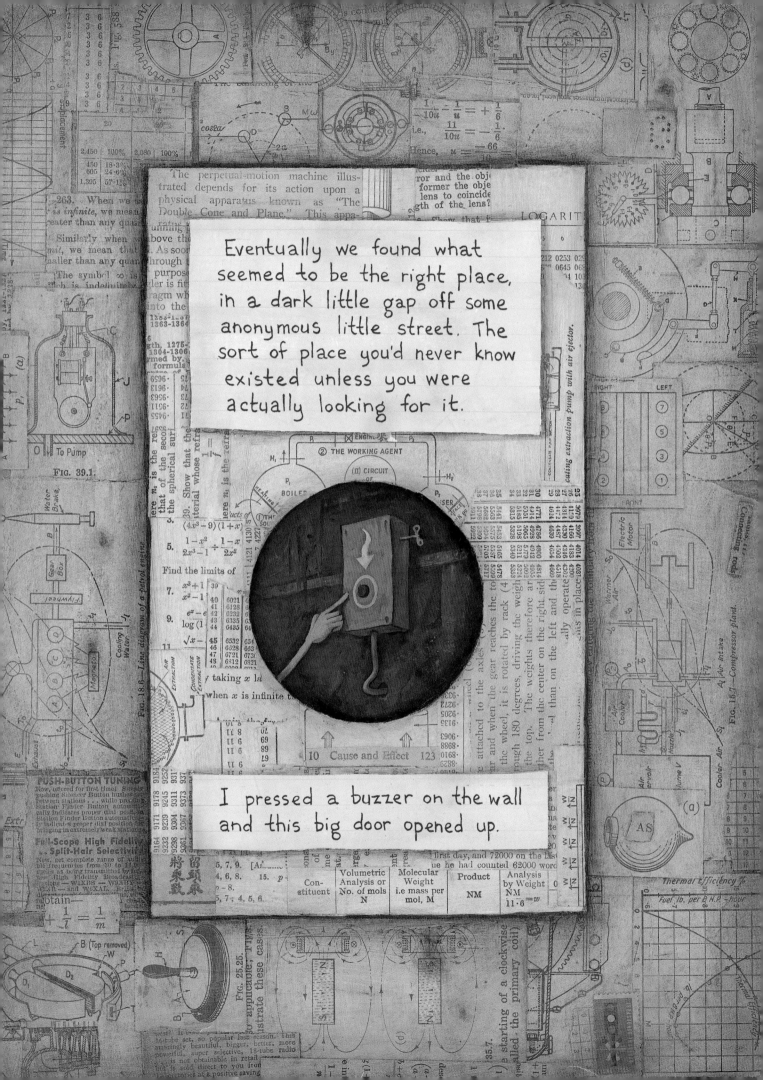

Eventually we found what seemed to be the right place, in a dark little gap off some anonymous little street. The sort of place you'd never know existed unless you were actually looking for it.

I pressed a buzzer on the wall and this big door opened up.

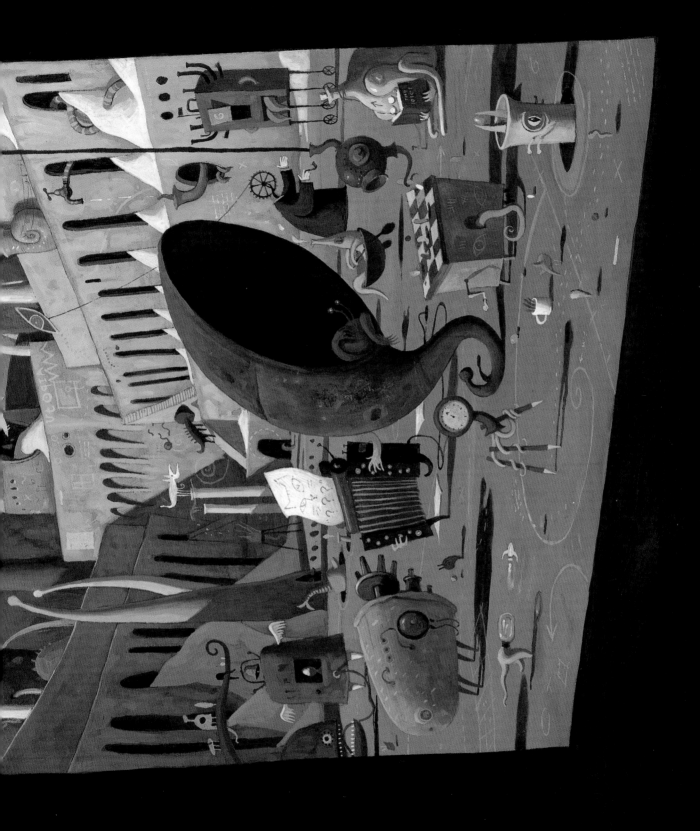

I didn't know what to think, but the lost thing made an approving sort of noise. It seemed as good a time as any to say good-bye to each other. So we did.

Then I went home to classify my bottle-top collection.

Well, that's it. That's the story.
Not especially profound, I know, but I
never said it was.
And don't ask me what the moral is.

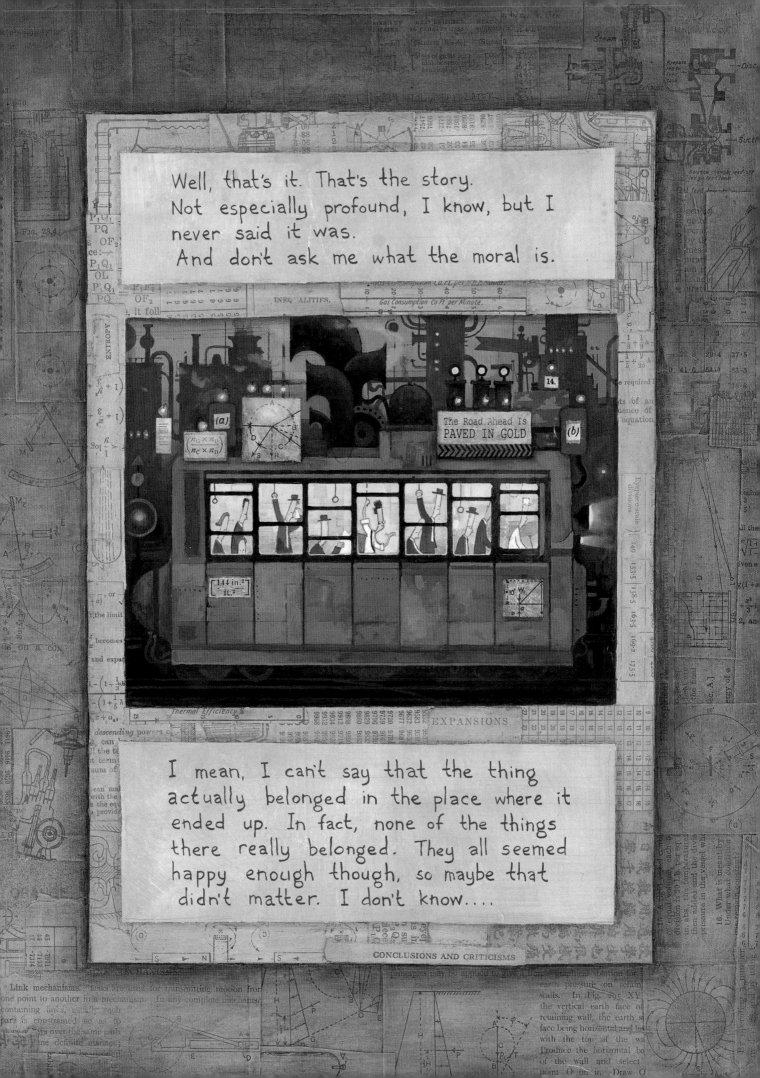

The Road Ahead Is
PAVED IN GOLD

I mean, I can't say that the thing
actually belonged in the place where it
ended up. In fact, none of the things
there really belonged. They all seemed
happy enough though, so maybe that
didn't matter. I don't know....

I still think about that lost thing from time to time. Especially when I see something out of the corner of my eye that doesn't quite fit.

You know, something with a weird, sad, lost sort of look.

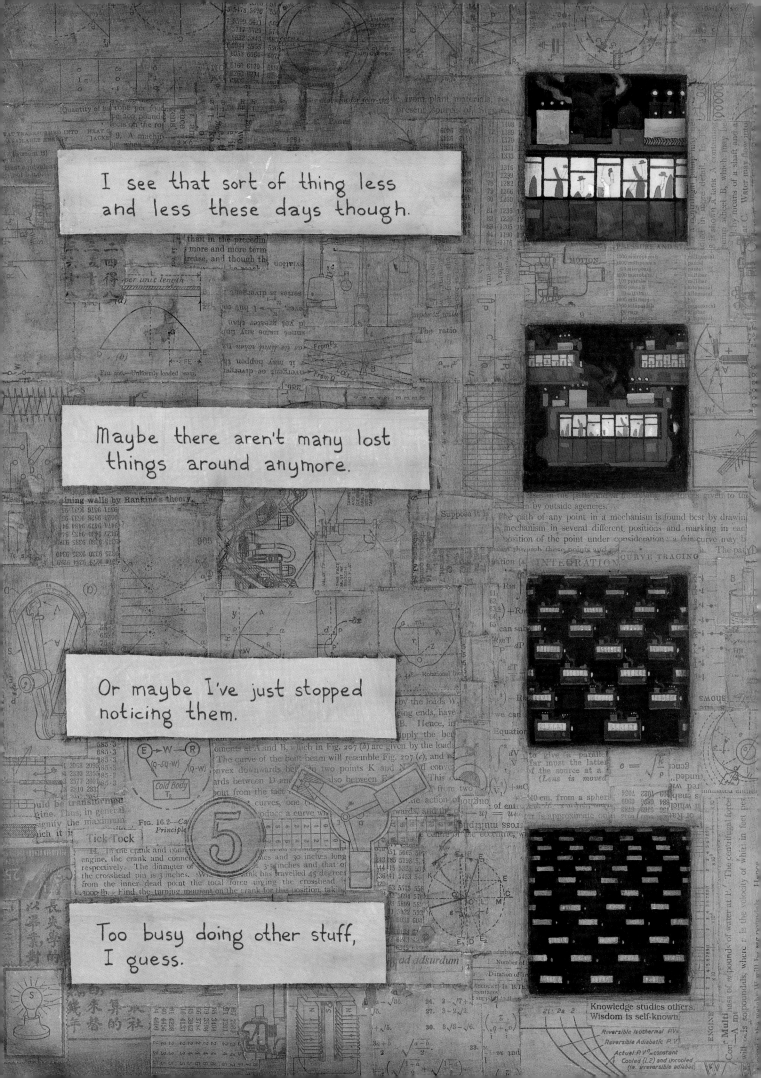

I see that sort of thing less and less these days though.

Maybe there aren't many lost things around anymore.

Or maybe I've just stopped noticing them.

Too busy doing other stuff, I guess.

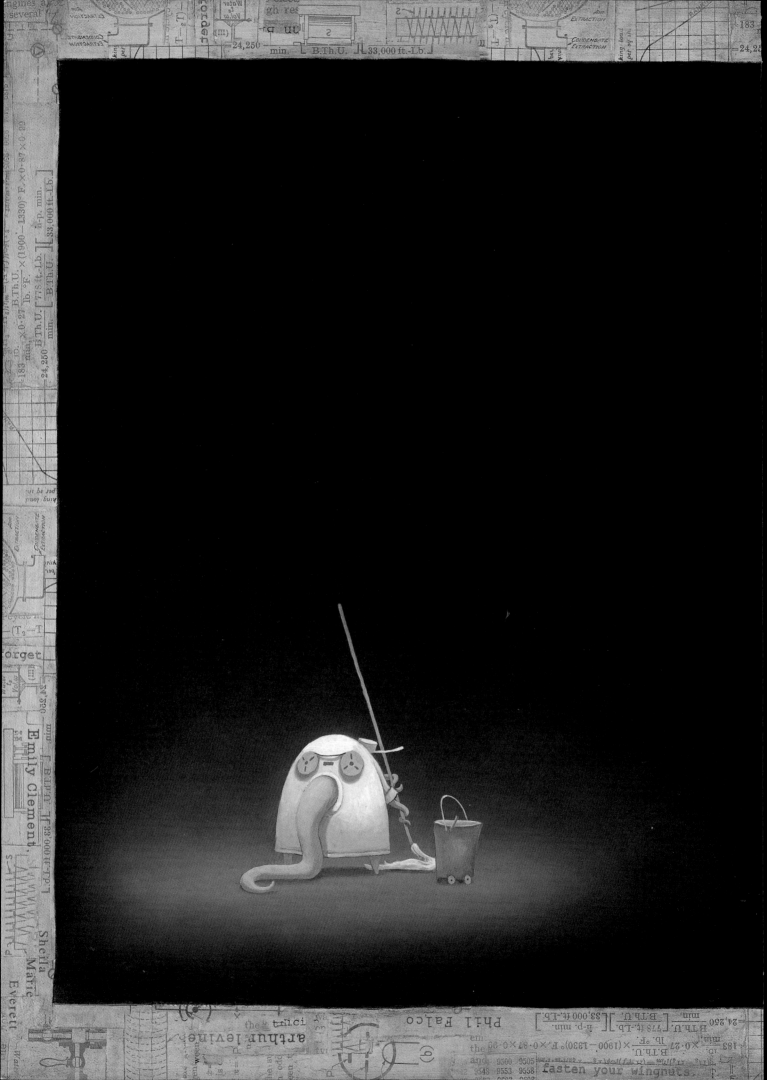

Edward Hopper

A John Brack

Jeffrey Smart

And APOLOGIES TO

Paul & The Twins.

The Funkmeister

Gary Crew

BILL DAY

the freo

centre folk,

it

Jonathan, Keira, Robin,

and for valued interest and comments from

with THANKS to   Helen Chamberlin   Chris D.   a fellow connoisseur of

heavy duty industrial plumbing

Editorial technician #264

The Rabbits   Words by John Marsden

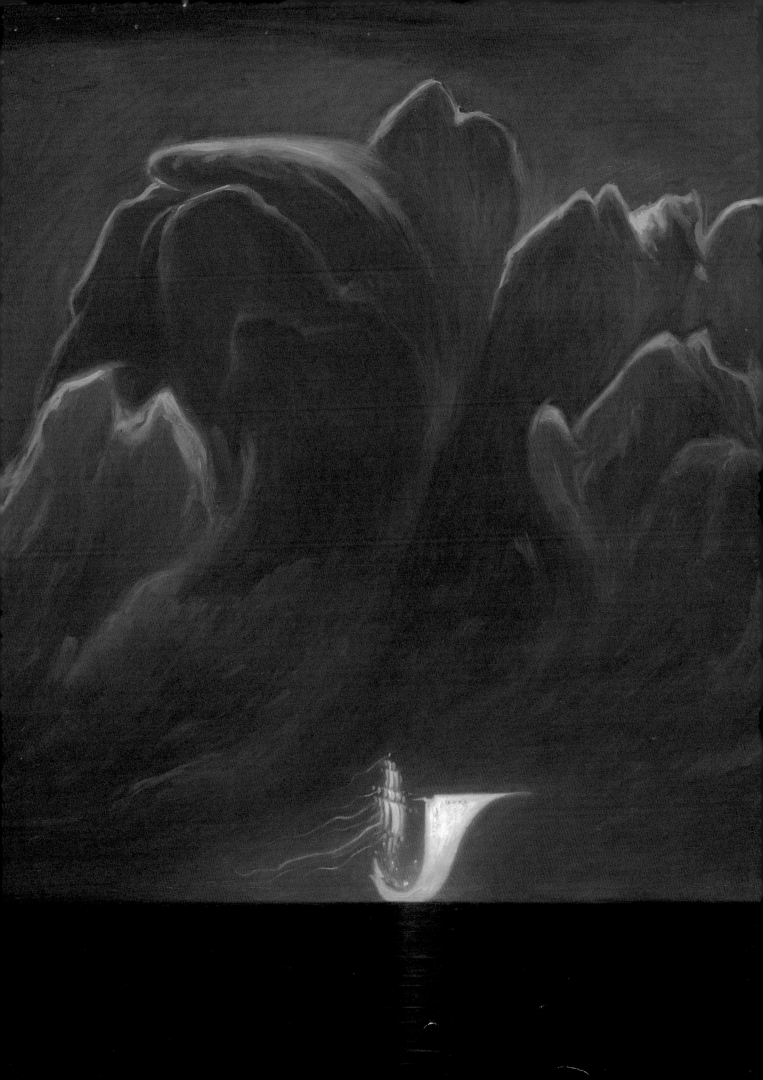

THE RABBiTS CAME MANY GRANDPARENTS AGO.

AT FIRST WE DIDN'T KNOW WHAT TO THINK. THEY LOOKED A BIT LIKE US.

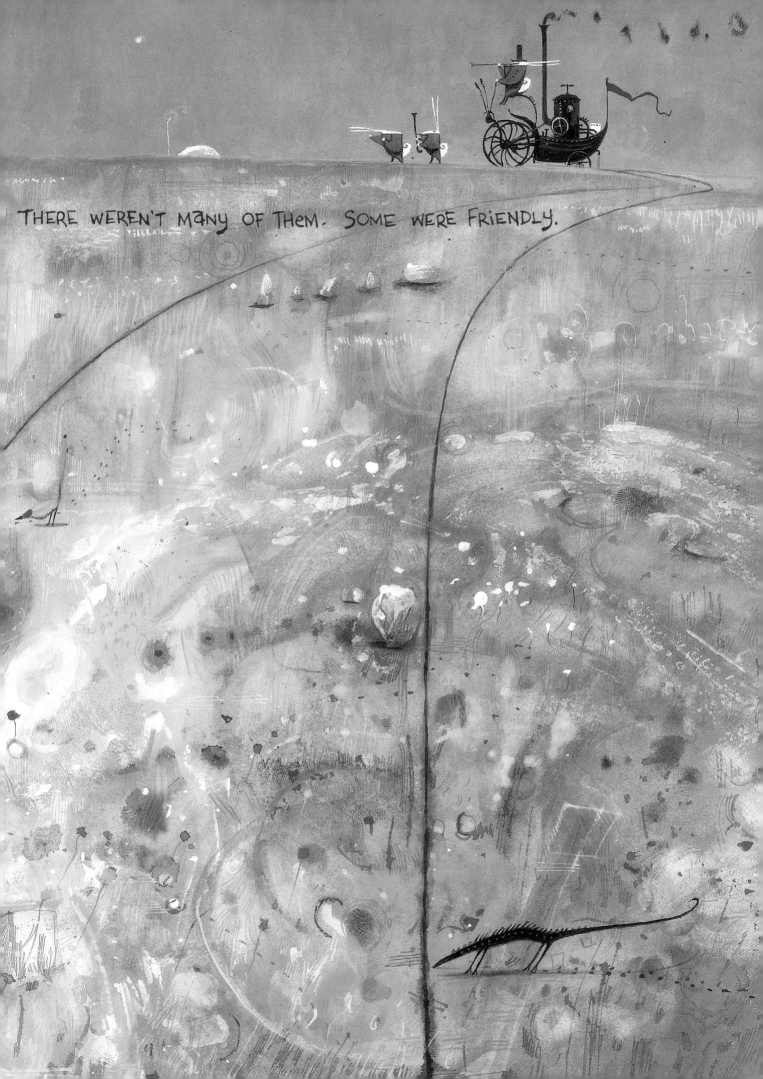

THERE WEREN'T MANY OF THEM. SOME WERE FRIENDLY.

MORE RABBITS CAME....

THEY CAME BY WATER.

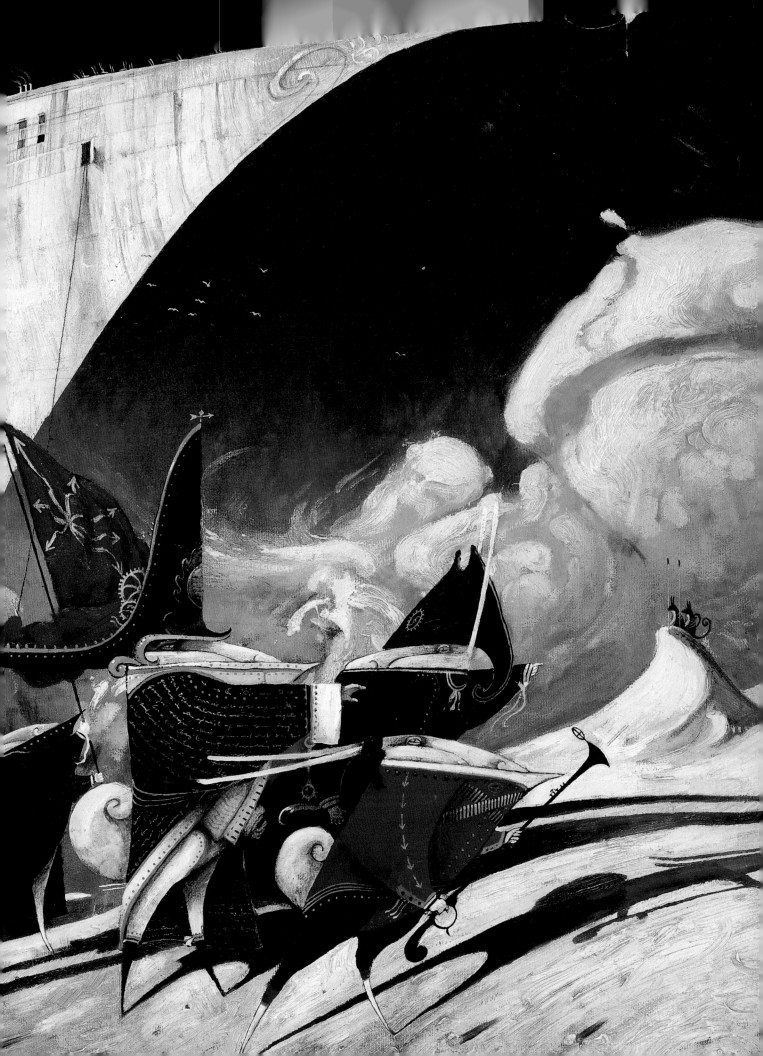

THEY DIDN'T LIVE IN THE TREES LIKE WE DID.

THEY MADE THEIR OWN HOUSES.

WE COULDN'T UNDERSTAND THE WAY THEY TALKED.

WE LIKED SOME OF THE FOOD AND WE LIKED SOME OF THE ANIMALS.

BUT SOME OF THE FOOD

MADE US SICK.

AND SOME OF THE ANIMALS SCARED US.

THE RABBITS SPREAD ACROSS THE COUNTRY.

NO MOUNTAIN COULD STOP THEM; NO DESERT, NO RIVER.

STILL MORE OF THEM CAME.

SOMETIMES WE HAD FIGHTS,

BUT THERE WERE TOO MANY RABBITS.

THEY ATE OUR GRASS.

THEY CHOPPED DOWN OUR TREES AND SCARED AWAY OUR FRIENDS...

RABBITS, RABBITS, RABBITS.
MILLIONS AND MILLIONS OF RABBITS.
EVERYWHERE WE LOOK THERE ARE RABBITS.

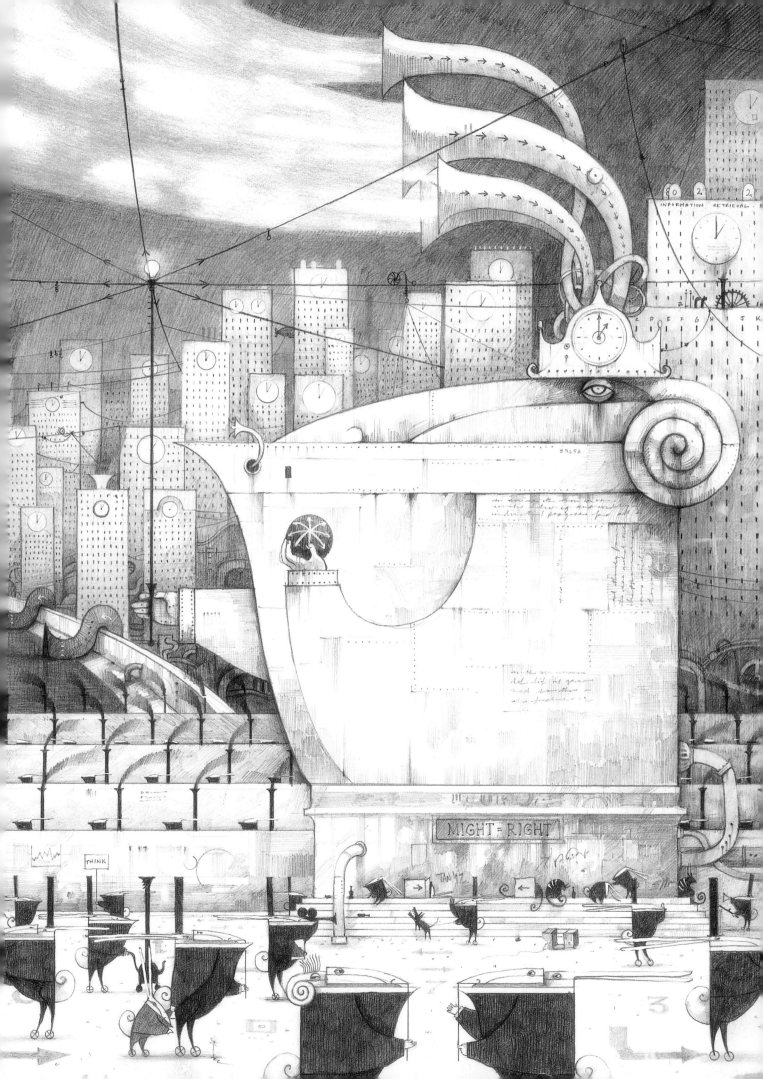